EPILOGUE

EPILOGUE

Notes from the End of the Line

How good we are, in theory, to the old: and how in fact we wish them to wander off like old dogs, die without bothering us, and bury themselves.
                                        Edgar Watson Howe

                                        Frank

Copyright © 2013 Frank Southwell

The moral right of the author has been asserted.

Apart from any fair dealing for the purposes of research or private study, or criticism or review, as permitted under the Copyright, Designs and Patents Act 1988, this publication may only be reproduced, stored or transmitted, in any form or by any means, with the prior permission in writing of the publishers, or in the case of reprographic reproduction in accordance with the terms of licences issued by the Copyright Licensing Agency. Enquiries concerning reproduction outside those terms should be sent to the publishers.

Matador
9 Priory Business Park,
Wistow Road, Kibworth Beauchamp,
Leicestershire. LE8 0RX
Tel: (+44) 116 279 2299
Fax: (+44) 116 279 2277
Email: books@troubador.co.uk
Web: www.troubador.co.uk/matador

ISBN 978 1780884 523

British Library Cataloguing in Publication Data.
A catalogue record for this book is available from the British Library.

Typeset by Troubador Publishing Ltd, Leicester, UK

Matador is an imprint of Troubador Publishing Ltd

Printed and bound in the UK by TJ International, Padstow, Cornwall

Overture	1
Intermezzo	35
The Fat Lady Sings	65
GLOSSARY	83

OVERTURE

The phone didn't ring today. No one knocked on the door to see if I needed help. That's not how it's supposed to be is it? When you're in sight of the finishing line, live alone and you're snowed in everybody rallies round – isn't that it?

Neighbour Derrick tells me that was how it used to be. Not sure myself. I was there too, a little before him in fact, but I don't remember it like that at all. We used to shout rude things and throw snowballs at grumpy old people when they complained. Derrick's a nice chap, wouldn't have done that, I'm sure. And by the way, he really is a Derrick which somebody ought to have told his parents is a kind of swivelling crane, getting its name from a seventeenth century hangman I believe. It probably suits him, a great advocate of capital punishment.

No, Derrick wouldn't have thrown snowballs, not at old people anyway. Derrick grew up in that lovely time when everybody behaved themselves. Well most, anyway. It couldn't have included me because I seem to remember doing things I probably wouldn't get away with now. And, come to think of it, there were a lot of other kids around who were rather frightening. They frightened me anyway. Oh, and there was an awful lot of dogshit about, *that* I can remember very clearly.

Derrick's my neighbour, at No.3. We're good friends really. He's got some long-handled loppers which I often borrow for pruning my trees. We occasionally have a drink together.

* * * *

Grown-ups keep telling me that childhood is the best time. Things must have changed because I spend a lot of time being frightened. It's hard to be good all the time and if I'm not all sorts of nasty things might happen to me. When I'm at home I have my mum and dad to worry about. When I'm at school there's the teachers — they give you the cane. And all the rest of the time there's God. He sees everything I do even when I'm in the lavatory and the door is shut. And you never know how God is going to punish you. There's a boy down the road who uses rude words all the time and he got seriously ill and nearly died. Now the Germans are dropping bombs on us I'm frightened we might get killed if we're bad. Some poor people in the old part of the town were killed the other night. I don't think they'll drop bombs on us here though, not in Grosvenor Park Avenue where I live. There are a lot of bad people in the old part of the town, so I expect God let the Germans drop bombs on them.

We call the Germans Jerries. I don't know why but we call chamber-pots jerries so perhaps it's meant to make us laugh at them and not be frightened. Anyway, the war is rather exciting, with lots of aeroplanes whizzing about, and guns and bombs making a lot of noise, mostly at night. When we go to school in the morning we look for bits of shrapnel and see who's got the biggest bit.

My dad's gone away now to fight the Germans. He hasn't got a spike on his helmet like the Germans have. It's so they know which side they're on.

* * * *

There's a lot of snow and ice about but nobody called to see if I needed anything, so after lunch I put on my hat and coat, also the boots I used to wear when I was going to go up mountains, then tottered and slithered on the icy pavement down to the nearby shops for a few essentials and a newspaper. I buy a newspaper for its crossword and the painless passing of time it affords me, that's all. There's no such thing as news for me any more because it's all happened before and I was there last time, even the time before that. Such experience ought not to be wasted. I've seen everything at least twice in my lifetime so it would be good sense for governments to ask me what they should not do, at least. "Can you tell us, Frank, why it all went belly up last time? We don't want to make the same mistake again." I don't want money, just feel I ought to be asked.

In my little suburban estate the newspaper of choice is the *Daily Mail*. It sells by the shelf-full because so many of us are getting on a bit and like it confirmed that the country is going to the dogs. There are nasty people out there, criminals and cheats, a lot of them foreigners, and we need to know. Derrick says we should send them back where they came from. This is an Anglo-Saxon country he insists. I don't know whether he is Anglo or Saxon, but his name is Morgan so a slip-up in the Repatriation Office could see him sent off to somewhere wet and unpleasant on the western fringes of whatever's left of the Empire. That would be a pity. He's a good neighbour, and lends me his tree-loppers whenever I need them. We often have a drink together. He seems to have a lot in common with my father who also thought that the country was going to the dogs. My father died fifty years ago so it occurs to me we should've arrived there by now – at the dogs I mean. I suggest to Derrick that if the country is going to the dogs at least most people now take their shit home and not leave it lying about.

* * * *

"Now that we know you're there Frank, with all that experience, perhaps you can help us with a few problems.

Like the community spirit – we don't seem to have it any more, not like we used to. People used to help each other out, get the shopping for the old folk, that sort of thing. When there was a problem everybody mucked in. How can we get that spirit back?"

Let's get it clear – who are these "we" you're referring to? I have to ask because if it's yourselves you mean, I was under the impression you still do help each other out, especially when it comes to jobs. No lack of community spirit there. If, as is more likely, your "we" is really referring to the remaining sixty million of us state-school graduates, it's not clear where your assumption of such a hallowed past is coming from. A master class in Catherine Cookson perhaps? You may even have made it up.

The community spirit I think you mean – in the rest of us that is – comes about when we're all in the same impoverished boat, when a lot of us are out of work and are filling in time, or when we are being bombed and have no house in the country to escape to. Burglary, widespread looting and even murder are all part of the community spirit in such times. Are you sure this is what you want?

* * * *

I buy the *Times* myself, a hangover from when I used to read the news. The *Daily Mail* crossword would probably pass the time just as well.

There's a coffee shop next to the newsagent's. On warm

days to pass more time I often sit outside with a cappuccino (I like the sprinkle of chocolate you get on top), watching my little bit of world going about its business. I like to look at women's legs even though much of the promise has faded. Once, I used to see a lot of people I knew but not any more. Perhaps they've all gone away somewhere, to live close to their now grown-up children, somewhere like that. That would be nice. One I know who's definitely gone away, was taken away, because he'd become a danger to the public. A bad case of dementia it was. Most likely many of them are dead. I watched one shake himself to bits with Parkinson's. Others I recognize, going down the shortening slope on sticks or embedded in wheelchairs, with vacant looks on their faces. Some I suppose don't go out any more, planning their day around silver strips of capsules and tablets, visits to the toilet, waiting for someone to get them up, put them to bed, empty their commode.

I don't know where cappuccino came from. One day we were all having coffee – April ninety-five I think it was – the next we were being asked, sir, which sort would you like…

As it's too cold to sit outside today, I pass up on the cappuccino and spend time in the chemist's instead. Over the shop front now it says "pharmacy" which sounds more trustworthy. I buy some ibuprofen for my lumbago. There's enough cures on those rows of shelves for everything and everyone. On one of them there's a capsule that'll keep me alive for ever – it's just knowing which is the right one. I've tried most of them but haven't yet identified the one that's kept me going so far. Like everyone else, I won't live long enough to find it I suppose. The trouble is every time I look there are new ones claiming to do the same thing only much better, so it looks as if I might have been wasting my time before. Then again, the one I'd last set my mind on – it was clear from the leaflet that immortality was a distinct possibility – has disappeared from the shelves.

There's a squashed cat in the road across from the shops. I wonder if it's Moses, the one that's been lost. There's a notice in the newsagent's window, and there's a small reward for any information. It doesn't say dead or alive though. Funny name for a cat, Moses.

* * * *

I think there must be a lot of German spies about, or shot down pilots. How would we know if we saw one? My mum says they don't have spikes on their helmets any more, and anyway they wouldn't be wearing helmets, would they? She says Germans have square features. I think Mr. Shipwell at No. 27 must be a German then, but I'm still allowed to play with his boys. If he is a German they don't seem to know that he's here. When the Messerschmidt swept down our road with its guns blazing we were all out in the garden. Or perhaps it missed us on purpose. Of course, there are sure to be good Germans, and Mr. Shipwell could very well be one of them, and that's why he is here and not over there.

My dad is in Africa, shooting at Germans, or maybe running at them with his bayonet. Back here we're fighting them ourselves, in the woods, every Saturday morning. We don't have guns and bayonets, so we fight them with bows and arrows, spears and swords cut from hazel shoots because they're straight. We never get to see the Germans because they run away before we get there, as you would expect them to do. They must know they're bad people. They must be very ashamed of themselves. I think if I was a German I'd give myself up, to our vicar the Reverend Parfitt, who would ask God to forgive me. I don't know about Italians though. The Pope is in charge of Italy, isn't he? You'd expect them to be good, although Italians are Catholic aren't they? worshipping idols, madonnas, that sort of thing, which the Reverend Parfitt tells us God doesn't like? No, I don't know about Italians. I've heard they're yellow. Not yellow like the Chinese, but yellow because they run away. Anyway, I'm not at all sure the Chinese are yellow. Mrs Lee down the street, on the other side – she's Chinese, you can tell by her eyes, and she's white as white can be.

When we are sure there are no more Germans in the woods we go home to dinner.

* * * *

"Frank, we're very concerned about the deteriorating standard of self discipline in the youth of today, their lack of respect for authority. With all your experience what can you suggest?"

Teddy Boys anyone? Remember them? Of course you don't – you government boys are barely out of short trousers, the ones we stopped wearing about the time our testicles descended and we stopped squeaking. Velvet collars, cut-throat razors and bicycle chains – that was us Teddies. We started in a small way, taunting the teachers, carving our initials on desk tops and taking potshots with our catapults at ducks on the municipal park pond. Later, as Mods and Rockers, on Bank Holidays we descended on coastal resorts for a good rampage along the beaches. How things have changed!

All right – I know, I know, it's not like that in other countries. The kids behave themselves, do as they're told. Tell them tomorrow we march into Poland and with a sieg heil they'll be off at dawn, boots glinting in the early morning sun.

Take your pick. It's one or the other.

* * * *

Why would anyone call a cat Moses?

When I get home I pass some time thinking about it. Perhaps the cat was found in a basket in a patch of bulrushes. That'd be stretching things a bit. Most likely it belonged to Jewish people, though I don't know of any round here. Derrick – he's my neighbour – might have nosed them out. Ho. If there is they'd be down on his list, so I'll keep quiet about the missing cat. The squashed cat will interest him though. It's a fate he would cheerfully wish on all cats, a notion I can have some sympathy with.

While I was out the postman has been. There's a letter from the doctor's telling me to go to the surgery for a flu jab. Suddenly, flu has become lethal and we need a jab, vulnerable people that is. Because I'm over sixty-five it seems I'm vulnerable, not an epithet I'm comfortable with. There's also a letter from Virgin urging me to take up their broad-band offer, something to do with the internet which I'm told is an essential for today's lifestyle. A bit like the trouser press used to be. I don't see trouser presses any more. Also amongst my mail is a plumber's bill. I called in the plumber because the central-heating boiler had cut out. It had cut out because the cold weather was too cold. Something had frozen up, possibly because the boiler had cut out. My father often used to tell me that I was too clever for my own good. I was never quite sure what he meant, but perhaps that's how my boiler is.

The last letter in the pile is an invitation to a re-union.

* * * *

"Frank, as you must be well aware, juvenile crime is on the increase. The kids are terrorizing the streets. What can we do about it?"

Juvenile crime isn't increasing. The age of juveniles is – it's what happens when you keep raising the school leaving age. There are juveniles, now, in their thirties. A juvenile is properly someone too young to go out and earn a living and take on a bit of responsibility. That, I suggest, is no older than fourteen by which time, if they're not very clever send them down the mines or up chimneys. OK, we don't have too many mines left, and that goes for chimneys too, but you get my drift. If at some later stage they develop a desire to study Sanskrit or the influence of the yurt on nineteen-thirties urban housing there's nothing to stop them.

* * * *

I want to be a Spitfire pilot. I often watch them whizzing about the skies chasing Messerschmidts before I'm dragged in and shoved in the cupboard under the stairs. The cupboard under the stairs is supposed to be the safest place in the house, and I've spent a lot of time in cupboards under stairs, but I think it's probably safer not to be in a house at all so you can see anything coming and run out of the way. And it's much more fun. Being a Spitfire pilot must be fun too, shooting down Germans. I wonder where the Germans go when they get shot down? We only pretend they're in our woods, but perhaps some really are. I don't think our pilots get shot down, just one here and there I suppose, but our pilots are so much better it can't happen very often.

When the all-clear goes we come out from under the stairs and go outside to see if we can see smoke coming up from anywhere.

* * * *

There's a squashed cat called Moses in the road by the shops. I don't know how I know it's called Moses. Someone must have told me.

The invitation to a re-union is from someone called Sprink. Can't think I've ever known anyone by that name but it seems he was in my Entry when I joined the RAF. Apparently a lot of those in the Entry that are still alive are getting together to celebrate the Diamond Jubilee of our enlistment. How they've found out where I'm now living is a mystery. I must have moved at least twenty times in those sixty years.

A funny business, this re-union lark, celebrating the past. As I remember it the past has often been pretty lousy, or I've done something in it that I'm not very proud of. When we all joined up we signed on for fourteen years, and didn't find out until the day afterwards that it wasn't where most of us wanted to be. Trapped, for fourteen years, in the custody of a punitive organisation dedicated twenty-four hours a day to eliminating any exhibition of normal individual behaviour — that was it if I remember rightly. Celebrate? Seems to me like celebrating the day you were sentenced for a crime you didn't commit. It looks very much as if there's a cell of elderly madmen out there that someone ought to keep an eye on. I don't want it to be me, although I do have a list of their names (which I shall keep for a bit) — our comrades, as Mr. Sprink puts it in his letter, an expression that strikes me as having an element of threat hanging about it.

Now I remember — the squashed cat wasn't called Moses. Well it might have been, but Moses was the lost cat in the newsagent's window. That was it.

* * * *

"The Statistics Office tells us, Frank, that five per-cent of the population leave school unable to read or write. What do you suggest we do?"

So what's new? Five per-cent sounds pretty good to me, as probably as good as it'll ever get. There are those out there who don't want to learn, have no intention of learning. Plenty make a pretty good living without being able to read or write – playing football or the guitar for example. And anyway we need people who can't read or write. People who read and write are inclined to aspire. If everybody aspires you'll find no-one to clean lavatories, that sort of thing. Five per-cent strikes me as being perfectly acceptable. Leave things alone. Don't fiddle.

* * * *

Hitler's only got one ball. We sing a song about it. He has a mate called Himmler who's only got one, too, and another mate called Goebbels who hasn't any at all. I wonder what happened, or perhaps that's how it is with Germans – we could ask Mr. Shipwell at Number 27 if Germans have trouble with their balls. It does seem to matter that you have balls because people laugh at Hitler and those other chaps, like if your front teeth stick out and you look goofy. Billy Godling looks like that and if you laugh at him and call him Goofy Godling he beats you up. Perhaps it's the same if you've only one ball. Or none at all. You beat people up.

Doodlebugs are exciting. They come in over the sea, very low and very fast making a noise like a motorbike, and with a flame coming out at the back. They're a kind of bomb. When they reach London they run out of fuel and come down and explode. Our planes are not supposed to shoot them down over the town but I suppose if they're not filled up properly they could stop and fall out of the sky anywhere. Did you know that the top speed of a Spitfire is three-hundred and ninety-seven miles an hour, but the doodlebugs go at four hundred? We now have a new fighter called a Tempest which can go faster to try and shoot them down before they get here. They shot one down over the sea last Sunday and it went in the front door of a church facing out to sea. After matins – that's the morning service. I know about such things because I am top boy in a choir and sing solos.

* * * *

I've had another letter from Mr. Sprink, Wg.Cdr Sprink as he still calls himself. It's all about the re-union that I missed. There's a photo of those who did turn up. Some relief. Pretty harmless they look, incapable of any mischief beyond parking in a disabled slot when they're not entitled to, which most of them probably are anyway. I mean, disabled badges are handed out like long-service medals these days, like something that's been earned, something you're proud to hold. I could probably get one myself. I expect I'm entitled to one – I've worked hard all my life. That's what you're supposed to say anyway.

Derrick's got a disabled badge. He had a replacement hip a few years back, but they never took his badge back.

The bungalow I live in was built in the nineteen-thirties. My father, a bricklayer, told me that houses built then were jerry-built, but they seem pretty tough to me. My electrician couldn't drill a hole in an inside wall in this one because the wall was built of a particular kind of tough brick once used for tunnels. Some of the houses round here have still got their original windows, not like those on the new estate next door – their windows didn't last twenty years. So maybe the country *is* going to the dogs. Funny expression that, going to the dogs, if you like dogs that is. Most dog people don't like cats – do they say going to the cats?

Can't stand dogs myself so it's all right. I don't like cats much either and nor does Dennis, my neighbour. There's a lot of cats round here – perhaps one of them is Moses. Odd name for a cat, Moses, the one that got squashed. Or lost. Even odder name I expect for today's people. They mostly won't ever have heard of Moses, will they? They won't be learning much about the Bible at school these days. I mean, it's the holy book of a bronze-age tribe, not much of an authority for the twenty-first century is it? We had it engraved on us. We learnt chunks of it word for word. I can tell you more about Moses than most kids can about that Harry Potter. Used to be able to anyway, though I can't be sure now because no-one asks me, and I've noticed I'm beginning to forget things.

My window-cleaner is called windolene.

* * * *

"We have too many people claiming benefits when they should be working, Frank. What's the answer?"

People like historians you mean – people like that? One man's salary is, after all, another man's benefits. The problem is all down to the British snob culture. What I think you mean is that you object to handing out taxpayers' money to support those who spend their time becoming experts on TV soaps and the phenomenon of celebrity culture when, for the same handful of peanuts, they could be sweeping the streets. Get your priorities right. We need street sweepers, so make street sweeping a well-rewarded and highly regarded career. The so-called benefit culture might just then disappear. You might even get historians joining the queue.

* * * *

Me and my mates, we're going to climb Mount Everest. Mount Everest is the highest mountain in the world and nobody's climbed it yet. In school we've been reading a book about it. There's not a lot of air up there so you have to have oxygen cylinders so you can breathe. There's four of us, and we're going to be the first ever to get to the top. They've agreed that I should be the leader. We're not quite old enough yet, but as I'm the clever one, top of the A class, I shall be leaving school as soon as I can to earn lots of money so we can buy ropes and oxygen cylinders and things.

A German bomber came over last week while we were at school.

The warning didn't sound and all of a sudden there were explosions. Bits of ceiling came down and we were rushed into the shelters which are under the boys' playground. After a little while a man covered in soot and with torn clothes came down and asked for his son. He told him it was no good going home because he hadn't got a home to go to — he must go to his grandma's. It was all very exciting. My mum came to meet us to take us home. She told us some houses just up the street had been flattened, along with the pie-shop and all the dogs were eating the pies. She wouldn't let us go and have look. We did the next day, though, on the way to school. There is a hole in the road at the back of the school.

* * * *

I meant to say my window-cleaner is called Simon.

Simon comes about once a month, probably a bit more than I need, but he does a good job and needs the money, and I wouldn't like to lose him. He's got a son called Josh, which I suppose is short for Joshua, but you can't be sure these days. Joshua fit the battle of Jericho. Hardly a battle, though, was it? They just shouted a lot and blew trumpets and the place fell down. Must've been jerry-built. Or Jericho built. Ho. If I remember rightly Joshua it was who took over from Moses, Moses the cat, and led his people to the Promised Land. It was supposed to be flowing with milk and honey. I wonder if it was, or where all the milk and honey went to. You don't hear anything about them now.

While I was at the hospital the other day — I went for an

audio test. I need to uprate my hearing aids, only they wouldn't give me the test because I had some earwax. They told me to go to my GP and get it removed. When I went to my GP the nurse – she's called a triage nurse now whatever that means – said I hadn't softened the wax first so I had to get working with the olive oil and go back three days later. This time she said that although the wax was now soft and she was a triage nurse she wasn't allowed to syringe my ear because I'd had a mastoidectomy sixty-six years ago, so I'd have to go back to the hospital to have the wax removed by specialist treatment. When I asked her to book me an appointment she said she was sorry but I would have to see the GP first for a referral, a matter of protocol. Now I've got to wait another week to see the GP so that he can make an appointment for me at the hospital to get the wax out of my ears. Then I can make an appointment at the hospital for my audio test. I think I've got it right.

My dad used to get the wax out of his ears with a matchstick.

Oh yes – I was saying that while I was at the hospital the other day, when I went for the audio test that I didn't have (I had earwax), I bumped into Alan – can't remember his surname – an old work colleague. For some years we knocked around together, went out for a drink once a week. He's a volunteer at the hospital, showing people where to go for what, very useful because it's one of those new hospitals the size of a small market town. They send you a map along with the letter of appointment. It even has its own buses. You can get lost very easily and if it wasn't for people like Alan you could be wandering around for days.

I shouldn't complain about the wax thing. The National Health Service mostly does a good job, a bit expensively sometimes though.

No, not Alan. Adrian, that was it.

* * * *

"Everyone's living longer. The pension cost is unsustainable, Frank. What on earth are we to do?"

Well, you can always scrap the National Health Service, let people die when their time comes. Mostly it'll be when they're no longer useful for the furtherance of the species or to the economy. Isn't that how it's supposed to be? A bit drastic though, and they'd have you out of office by the end of the week. No, do nothing. This living longer thing is a demographic blip. We have a new breed destined for the early bath – teeming hoards of fat people, indolent people, alcoholic people, people who don't eat their greens, and druggies out there who're going to keel over long before their pensions kick in, just like most of us used to. Hold your nerve. It won't be long.

* * * *

I've got a new team together, to go to the South Pole. We've been reading a book about Captain Scott. No one British has got there and back alive yet and we're going to be the first. You have to have dogs. Captain Scott had horses and that's where he went wrong. It's going to be difficult because dogs don't like me – they chase me and bite. I've passed the scholarship and am going to the Grammar School, so I'll get a good job with lots of money to pay for the dogs and the boat to get to there. The others have to stay on at this school until they are fourteen when they start work, ordinary work, but they won't be getting much money, so it's up to me. I haven't made up my mind yet which we're going to do first, Mount Everest or the South Pole.

The war has just finished. Lots of people had street parties, poor people I think because their houses are too small to have parties in and they don't have jelly very often. We didn't have a street party. I think we're poor but I think we don't think we're poor because we live on an avenue not a street which is where poor people live. I never heard of anybody having an avenue party.

If there were Germans in the woods they won't be there now. Anyway, there are some out on the streets, let out from the prisoner of war camp across the fields. My dad – he's back from the war now – invited two in for Sunday dinner. One was named Otto. They didn't seem to have square heads.

* * * *

This morning I went down to the chemist's for my whatsit, prescription. The Chemist's called a pharmacy now. I suppose they think it sounds more important. They still sell the same things and do predictions –

prescriptions. I should've gone yesterday, but I forgot, so I went without my pills today. I'm still here though, so they can't be that important

I'm on the Tumbrel myself, for blood pressure. High blood pressure, that is. It's like weather. These days weather means bad weather. On TV anyway. There's some weather coming in off the Atlantic this weekend, they say. So people say they've got blood pressure. Actually it's the Tumbiril what I'm on – not the Tumbrel which I might be on pretty soon if I don't take them. Ho. Anyway, this Tumbiril stuff dilates the arteries, which baffles me. If you know anything about fluid dynamics at all you'll know all about the venturi effect – when a passageway is restricted flow speeds up and pressure drops, and vice-versa. I raised this with my GP. I told him that if the Tumbiril dilates my arteries my blood flow slows down and the pressure rises, not drops. He didn't know about the venturi effect, so now he says he's baffled too. It seems to work though. Perhaps it's the placebo effect.

They've taken the notice about Moses – the squashed cat – out of the newsagent's window, so perhaps he's been found.

The capsules – the ones I take for my blood pressure, high blood pressure – come in silver strips with the days of the week marked alongside them. They start the week on Sunday, which seems odd. Perhaps the company who makes them is owned by someone with a name like my window cleaner, Simeon, someone who thinks the week ends on Saturday. Simeon, son of Jacob, – see, I still remember my Bible. Had it engraved on us we did, the holy book of a pre-historic desert tribe who lived on dates and camels' milk. Oh, and manna. You won't know what that is, and I can't be bothered to explain.

Simon, not Simeon, my window-cleaner's name.

I know desert tribes lived on dates and camels' milk because I've read Doughty's *Travels in Arabia Deserta.*

Another thing I forgot yesterday – it was my daughter's birthday. I forgot the card. She lives down south. I'll have to telephone tonight. After six-o'clock it's cheaper.

* * * *

"Frank, what on earth are we going to do about Afghanistan? Our brave soldiers are getting killed."

First things first. Soldiers get killed when you go to war. When you sign up to being a soldier, there's a good chance it might kill you. I'm not quite sure where the brave bit fits in. It sounds too much like a conscience thing. Best leave it out.

Now about Afghanistan. What on earth do they teach you in history at school these days? YOU DON'T DO ANYTHING ABOUT AFGHANISTAN. Nobody has been able to do anything about that chunk of the world we call Afghanistan, EVER – go and take a look and you'll realise why. If you were a town council you'd allocate a street somewhere in the town for those bloody awkward nuisance people that you can't do anything with. For your town think World. For the street think Afghanistan.

Oh, and while you're at it, encourage people to buy poppies as cut flowers. That way they'll never run to seed.

* * * *

Don't like the Grammar School. It's too strict, much more frightening than the other school. You get the cane for so many things, like not wearing your cap or not doing your Latin homework properly. Did you know that Latin verbs have tenses, like pluperfect? My maths master is very short and terrifies us. Some of the masters have a thing called shell-shock which they got in the last war and have peculiar habits. One of them suddenly starts throwing things about. The other day he tried to throw a desk across the classroom. We have another one who has one leg shorter than the other, which makes him angry all the time because he couldn't go to war and get shell-shock like the others. That's what I heard someone say anyway.

There's a mysterious place in England somewhere called Kinder Scout. I've read about it in the papers. People go there and just disappear. A plane has done it too, just disappeared. Sounds exciting, especially with a name like that. Now I'm at the Grammar School I don't see my Mount Everest and South Pole friends any civilized conduct has developed from the philosophy of an elite living in a fruitful landscape with lots of tasty pieces of meat running around. It ain't like that where they come from, never has been. So who's right? You should worry that their holy book is much younger than yours, and so might just be a bit more up to date in its ideas. So stop preaching about your version of civilization. And for God's (or Allah's) sake shut up about human rights.

Oh, and you might try a bit harder at finding an alternative to oil.

* * * *

The big trouble with the Grammar School is that there are no girls. Girls who pass the scholarship go to the High School, a couple of miles away. A pity. Luckily there are girls in the choir and in the church youth club. Being top boy and singing solos was a big help in getting their attention, but it's not so easy now my voice has broken.

I've started a cycling club in my class. There's six of us so far. We plan to do a bit of exploring. I couldn't ride a bike so they took me out on Tuesday night to teach me.

My dad thinks it's good that I've learned to ride, and he'll try and find the money to buy me a bike. Before the war he had to cycle all the way up to London every week for work, laying bricks. That's sixty miles. I hope to be able to do that. If I'm going to climb Mount Everest and go to the South Pole or open up Kinder Scout that's the least I ought to be able to do, once I've stopped wobbling. Tomorrow we're going on a five mile run. That's a start.

My birthday's next month so I might get my bike then. The problem is that they'll be buying me long trousers because I'll be fourteen, and so might not have enough money left to buy the bike as well.

* * * *

I didn't go for a flu jab. Never had flu so I suppose I'm immune. My wife Margaret never had flu either. Never had a day in bed up to the day she died nearly three years ago. Derrick had a flu jab last year and was down with pneumonia within the week. There doesn't have to be a connection of course, but I'm hearing a lot of tales along those lines. Which flu the jab is for I'm not sure – there's a whole host of flus and they come in skeins. I think that should be strains. Geese come in skeins. So does wool. Did. Wool comes in balls these days.

We're told that some of these flus are pretty serious. A few years back we had bird flu which was ready to wipe out civilization. It didn't get a hold over here. There was a parrot imported that might have had it, if I remember. Then there was a dead duck somewhere up in Cumbria that turned out to have died from lead poisoning from fishing weights. Then we had swine flu, another threat to civilization. I think that one's still doing the rounds, quietly killing off the odd pensioner with breathing difficulties. There was one flu just after the first world war that killed millions. Came from Spain, if I remember rightly. There must be others we don't know about yet, lurking round the corner. Badgers perhaps. They have TB don't they?

Yes, wool comes in balls now. When it came in skeins I used to have to sit for hours with it looped over my hands while Margaret wound it into a ball. I don't know why it came in skeins. Margaret never had flu so, like me, she never bothered with the jab. Derrick had the jab and got pneumonia.

* * * *

"We'd love to find an alternative to oil, Frank, but people don't seem to like wind farms. They worry about nuclear power, and if we suggest barrages the bird people go bananas."

You were elected to run the country weren't you? Well run it then, like governments used to when they put up telegraph poles and electricity pylons and doused us daily in carcinogens from coal-fired power stations. You've even got a valid excuse. It's either war over oil and lots of people getting killed – or wind farms. Or nuclear plants. Or barrages. Or whatever.

Ignore the nimbies, the slightly mad royals and the small handful of very comfortable, mostly bearded, people who claim to have their country's best interests at heart. They don't, only their own, including the hope of sainthood. Anyway, they'll be the first to jump on you when the lights go out and the bombs go off down their street – sorry, Avenue. What's more in a hundred years' time it'll be their progeny who'll be making all the fuss about our industrial heritage when someone tries to take a turbine down.

And what on earth is this problem that all you governments seem to have with bird people? Bird-watching is trainspotting for snobs. Did anyone take any notice of trainspotters when the noble Beeching wielded his axe and chopped out ten thousand miles of branch lines? The birds'll find somewhere else or evolve a bit if barrages don't suit them. It's what they've been doing for millions and millions of years. Anyway there'll be birds up there we've never seen just dying for a nice barrage to settle down in.

* * * *

Hate school. Spend all my time avoiding the cane, and sports. The Housemaster put my name down for the school cross-country. I achieved a small measure of fame by coming in sixth for the House, the last to count. As I was one-hundredth-and-tenth it was no surprise our House came last. Of course, it would be different if I was doing something I really wanted to do. Like the South Pole. Or Everest. In two years time I take the School Certificate. Don't really know what you do with the Certificate when you've got it. I suppose it helps you to get a good job and earn lots of money. I don't know how you go about this Pole and Everest business. It's not a job is it? "Wanted — enthusiastic young man to join our team in its attempt on Mount Everest, well paid, must have School Certificate." No, I don't think it's like that.

Took my cycling club up to Herne Hill last Saturday to watch the national sprint championships, in particular Olympic champion Reg Harris — I could be like him. Actually, only one turned up and he'd had enough by half way, so he went back home. There's a lot of hills in the Weald and the North Downs, and I thought of my dad struggling over them each way every week with his trailer on the back of his bike. Now he's dying – his stomach. Someone said it's what you get from eating a lot of tinned food like the soldiers were fed on in the war. Apparently he's only got six months. I don't know what I think of him dying. He's not been around for so much of my life that perhaps I won't miss him. I'm supposed to, aren't I?

* * * *

The bin-men didn't come round today. Either that or they missed mine which would be surprising because they're usually very punctilious. They come on Wednesdays, early, so I put the bin out last night but it hasn't been emptied. I'll leave it out just in case. Derrick, next door, must've got his days mixed up because he's only just put his out.

There's a lot of flu around. Didn't bother with the flu jab myself, never do. Margaret, my wife, never did either. She died three years ago, nearly four now. If it ain't broke don't fix it, she used to say. She wouldn't have HRT when all women over fifty were being told they should have it; you shouldn't muck about with natural processes she said. And we know now she was right. Next it was statins that everybody should be having, for cholesterol. We know where that led, don't we? I keep wondering about the Tumbiril I'm taking. It's for blood pressure – high pressure, that is. It dilates the arteries. Makes me sneeze. Most of my colleagues are on the same stuff. God knows where that's taking us all.

Which reminds me – I have to renew my prescription. I'm on Tuesday's capsule and they run out on Saturday. I think it was Tuesday's capsule – not sure, hadn't got my glasses and the print is very small. I need some new glasses anyway. Out walking the other day I mistook a cart for an elephant, and some weeks back I was attacked by a duck that turned out to be a white carrier-bag blown at me by the wind.

Don't know why Saturday is the last day on the strip. You'd think it would be Sunday wouldn't you? Would be fine of course for anyone called Isaac, Sabbath people. Remember Isaac? Son of Abraham, the one Abraham was ready to kill off when God told him to. Nice dad. Nice God too, that one. And he's still about, in some places. I don't have a God myself but it's pretty obvious that if you insist on having a God, you need to choose carefully.

Just thought – if I'm on the right capsule it's Tuesday and that's why my bin hasn't been emptied. And why Dennis has just put his out. They come round tomorrow then, Wednesday. Derrick. Don't know why I've started calling him Dennis. If I think of a swivelling crane I won't go wrong.

* * * *

"Frank, the people don't seem to trust us. They think we're all a lot of self-seeking megalomaniacs, and that's not fair. What can we do?"

My my! What's all this about fairness? Isn't that what spoilt children say? Let's face it – you *are* self-seeking megalomaniacs. If it wasn't already in your genes, you were almost certainly schooled very expensively in the business of self-seeking megalomania, which should have dawned on you not later than your first erection in the dorm. There comes amongst you the occasional Christ it's true but a similar fate, if not quite as brutal, is usually in store.

So cut out the innocence. The "people" as you call us have no alternative but to accept that their choice is between one of you megalomaniacs and another. We are sometimes fooled by the lowly born and reared, so if you want to be seen as belonging to the rest of us, try being poor. Really poor, that is, going without jelly, that sort of thing.

* * * *

I've taken my School Certificate, think I did all right. Not sure about the French Oral though. The examiner showed me a pictorial map of Paris – I think it was Paris – and pointed to a tall smoking chimney with a postage stamp beside it. Qu'est-ce que c'est? he asked. Je ne sais pas, I told him. C'est un facteur de timbre poste, he explained. I really don't know about such things. I've never seen a factory. I didn't think that little things like stamps needed big things like smoking chimneys to make them.

In a month's time I leave school and have to start work. No-one's told us anything about work or where it comes from, so I've no idea what I'll be doing. I don't even know what I want to do, and nobody's asked me or suggested anything. A man came to the school the other day and gave us an interesting talk about an RAF technical college where people were trained to become highly qualified engineers. I don't really know what engineers do, but I'm curious about how things work and know a little about engines so perhaps I could be an engineer. And if you're going to be an engineer, aeroplanes would be exciting.

Anyway, if I get my Certificate I should be able to get a good job. One of my friends got his School Certificate last year and got a job in the Borough Treasurer's Office which sounds pretty important so he should do well. I don't know how he got it. At the moment he has the job of going round collecting all the pennies from public toilet doors, but of course you have to start at the bottom, I can see that.

* * * *

INTERMEZZO

I shan't be borrowing Derrick's tree-loppers any more. The handles are about ten feet long which makes them very unwieldy, and last time I used them I overbalanced and ended up face down in the rose bed. Don't like roses much myself, but the bed was Margaret's and I can't bring myself to get rid of them, just let them run wild like the rest of the garden. I mow the lawn, that's about it. A chap called Ruby comes round once a month and does a bit. I'll get him to do the trees. Funny name for a man. Short for Ruben I suppose. Or Reuben – isn't that how it's spelt? Son of Jacob wasn't he? Used to know them all.

Dennis is a Lion. Derrick I mean – I have to think of a swivelling crane. He's a Lion. Lions are good people who go round raising money for charity. He was down at the shops today, wearing a top hat and cranking a barrel-organ, collecting for the annual flood-fest in Bangladesh. I don't seem to see any Lionesses. Perhaps they're at home doing the ironing. Always wary of man things myself – rugby club stuff, male voice choirs, that sort of thing. Not normal is it, when the business we're supposed to be about is procreation?

I've got some new hearing aids. Digital. Everything's digital now. Digital good, analogue bad. Everything except watches – they didn't last long, did they?

That business with the tree-loppers – when I fell over in the rose bed – it's a confidence thing. Can't stand on a chair to change a light bulb these days. Last time I tried I went all wobbly, grabbed the flex and pulled the light fitting out of the ceiling. Had to get a man in. Once I was going to climb Mount Everest, go to the Pole, sail single-handed round the world, fill up the Empty Quarter. Now I can't change a light bulb. Mind you, there doesn't have to be a connection. Could Tensing change a light bulb? or Scott? We'll never know. I mean Tensing wouldn't have had light bulbs would he? – just a candle made out of some part of a yak. And Scott – even if he had light bulbs he'd have had someone from below stairs up to change his.

* * * *

"Now you've mentioned the Pole Frank, all that melting ice is going to swamp London. And other places of course, although most of those are not our concern unless they have oil. We understand it's something to do with climate change and we're to blame. What can we do?"

Nothing. Nothing is what you can do. Don't you know there's always been climate change? Planet Earth jiggles about a bit so temperatures go up and down, sometimes seriously. I can't quite speak from experience but if it wasn't a lot hotter in these parts in Roman times Hadrian's wall would've been a non-starter. Not so very long before that the London you're so worried about was just a big block of ice. Anyway, last time sea-levels rose we ended up with the Channel, and what a blessing that's turned out to be.

* * * *

I'm on janks, seven days – punishment in the RAF for not doing what you're told or not coming up to scratch on inspection. On janks you get six inspections, an hour of manic drill on the parade ground, washing-up in the cookhouse, all squeezed into the already fraught every-day routine. At my very first inspection on janks I got charged for a "dirty" cap-badge. It looked pretty shiny to me, but I think they just wanted an excuse. On balance I think I preferred the cane – all over and done with in one go.

There's a good chance at this rate I'll never get off. And I've another fourteen years to go – signed up for by me and agreed by my mum and dad. All I had to do was pass a little exam, do a few aptitude tests, and have a medical check to see if I had otitis-media or an undescended testicle. You can't help feeling proud to know that you don't have an undescended testicle, so here I am. See where pride gets you? Having an undescended testicle can't be that bad, can it?

The all-seeing God I used to worry about has been replaced by a twenty-four-hours-a-day military machine just as keen on punishment, except it doesn't care if I swear so long as it's at someone of my own or lesser rank. Nil Illegitemae Carborundum – don't let the bastards wear you down, that's what we say. There's a multi-tiered hierarchy of them – bastards that is – and I'm right at the bottom. The top half of the hierarchy is made up mostly of cocky little ex public-school boys, now called Officers, who seem to think that the rest of us are untutored peasants straight out of the fields. That's not what I, a cocky little grammar-school product, puts up with easily. We have to salute them. The other day I forgot, which is why I'm here, on janks.

Apparently if you're going to be a highly qualified engineer you must also have razor-sharp creases in your trousers, have boots like mirrors, keep your hair at least one inch clear of your ears, and be able to execute a bayonet charge. There are lots of other requirements, some of which I expect I'll find a use for when I start work on aircraft. Like being able to file a block of mild steel down to within plus or minus two-thousands of an inch of a prescribed measurement. And getting covered in engine oil. I'm pretty good at that but near the bottom of the class when it comes to doing things to bits of metal.

The other week one of us was found to have TB, and is going to be discharged. What luck! Well, we're not sure really, but when the rest of us were checked and found to be clear there was an air of disappointment in the ranks – I think they can cure TB these days. A few weeks back one chap ran away to Southern Ireland, but they caught him and brought him back. He's in a cell in the Guardroom now, and they've taken away his braces and bootlaces in case he tries to hang himself. The very clever chap who sits next to me in classwork has started limping, although I don't think there's anything really wrong with his leg. When he reported sick they told him he was malingering and threatened to charge him. He's still limping.

* * * *

My latest hearing aids are digital. Clever stuff. They can be programmed to match your specific needs, the audiologist told me. She had nice legs. Poppy, that's what it said on her label, name-tag, badge. These days everybody has labels. Poppy. "Hello, I'm Poppy – what shall we call you?" How about Daffodil? Or Scott of the Antarctic? We used to keep our distance. Still, it's a nice name – Poppy. And very appropriate just now because it's that time again, when you're not supposed to forget or the Poppy Police will mark you down as a nasty person.

They start wearing them earlier every year – the TV people get in first, a fine show of care for us all to follow. I wonder if Poppy's wearing her poppy. Stopped wearing one myself – can give you six reasons why if you want. I drop the odd coin in the box of course, helps to pay for a wooden leg or two, that sort of thing. Ho. My neighbour – the one with the name like a swivelling crane, Derrick – will be wearing his. Poppy, that is, not wooden leg. Derrick the Lion. He's a Legionnaire too, British that is. He'll be out there on parade on Sunday, marching with the rest of the silly old show-offs with their medals jangling. Still, I can't see this tomfoolery lasting much longer. Today's people don't know how to march, wouldn't know where to begin. Good thing too. Teach people to march, give them a rousing tune and off they'll go to wherever you point them, including war. Einstein despised them. Nice to know I'm up there with some of the greats.

Dennis bought all of his medals – got them on the internet. He had flat feet so they didn't even allow him in for National Service. I'm not supposed to know that but his son told me.

Picked up a real headache from somewhere. I'll have a couple of Papermates and lie down for a bit. Peppermints. No. Paracetamols, that's it. Paracetamol.

* * * *

"What are we going to do about all these protesters, Frank? How on earth do we stop them wrecking the place?"

Bus in as many brass bands as you can and get them to play martial music. Before you know where you are the ancients will be lining up in formation and marching off anywhere you choose the bands to take them. The nearest cliff might be a good idea. It'll help too if you give them all a few medals to wear. For those younger ones unfamiliar with the business of marching and the idea of an orderly society it shouldn't be too difficult, a little bit of TV programme rescheduling – an all-day episode of a popular soap, say, when a brush with bubonic plague sees most of the characters breaking out in lumps and dying horribly. All you'll have to deal with then is a handful of people in balaclavas, looking silly and trying to slink off home.

* * * *

This is my story, this is my song
We've been in this Air Force too bloody long......

... just something we sing, especially when drunk. I'm now three up from the bottom of the hierarchy. Doesn't make any difference, the posh boys are still there, the Officer Classes. Still think they're destined to rule, us to look after them, not at all happy about this idea that we should all be educated. "Nice to see you taking an intelligent interest Corporal", said one the other day as he picked out Tennyson on my bookshelf during inspection. You can see why I sometimes want to hit them. In bad times I get drunk and play Chopin. Oh yes, I play Chopin. Beethoven too. They don't know that. They know I've got Latin and that worries some of them enough.

I once thought being a highly qualified engineer working on aircraft would be exciting. About four years ago it was. People would look up to me and think "wow". Well, they don't. They have a pretty poor view of anyone called an engineer. And being in the armed forces pitches you even lower down the scale. They may have a point there, when we go out on the beer, smash things up and fight it out with the local blokes who think we're pinching their women.

Ah, yes. Women. That's what life is really about I've discovered. One in particular just now, got great legs, really fancy having her around long-term. Where the hell's my vision of leading a team up Everest gone? Anyway it's been done now, by this bloke with a woman's name and a Sherpa which I thought was some kind of a pack animal but turned out to be a local guide, a little weather-beaten chap with a squashed face. I still fancy the Pole, mind you – you can get there on caterpillar tracks these days, but to do it properly you have to slog it out on foot.

I don't know how I got into this, and I've no idea how I get out of it. I could try limping, like the chap who used to sit next to me when we were apprentices. He made it in the end, medical discharge. Sheer persistence. Clever bugger he was, much cleverer than me.

* * * *

I don't play Chopin any more. Or Schubert. Or Beethoven. Or the others. Tinnitus. And I've got hearing aids, digital ones. I put it down to all those days on the rifle range, banging away with a piece of equipment pre-dating the Boer War. Well, almost. We didn't have those things you wear over your ears then, or if we did nobody mentioned them. Anyway we wouldn't have worn them, not us tough Brits.

Julian, across the road, has hearing aids like me, but he's only in his fifties. He used to drill holes in roads and didn't wear things over his ears. I can understand that – a chap called Julian working on the black stuff, digging up roads, isn't going to wear things over his ears is he? You might just get away with it as a Bert. I rather fancy Julian's wife Rita. A keen gardener, gardeness, she's got great legs. I like to watch her weeding, bending down.

Ear-defenders – that's it. Ear-defenders. No, we didn't have anything like that. They came in with health and efficiency. Health and safety, I mean. Health and Efficiency was a naturist magazine we used to buy because it was full of photos of naked women playing badminton, that sort of thing. Dennis got away with it, never had to fire a rifle. He didn't have to do National Service because he had flat feet, and you can't march properly with flat feet. I'm not supposed to know that, but his daughter told me. He bought all his medals on the internet.

No, I don't play Chopin any more. Thinking about it, I don't know why I played Chopin when things got bad. All that minor-key stuff's guaranteed to get you reaching for the bottle at the best of times. When you're wallowing in self pity there's nothing like a bit of the *Ballade in G Minor* or *Fantasie in F Minor* to push you under – OK so the *Fantasie* drifts into A Major, but that's what does it for me. I don't get drunk any more either, though I went at it a bit when Margaret died, four years ago. I still miss her a lot.

Come to think of it the Boer War wasn't so long ago *then* – when I was banging away on the rifle range – as *then* is from *now*. Jesus! am I that bloody old?

* * * *

"Frank, we seem to have this obesity problem. We keep urging people to eat more healthily but nobody takes any notice. There's a time bomb ticking away. What can we do?"

If that's the royal "we" you're talking about, it's hardly noticeable. Just cut back on the carbohydrates. But what I think you really mean is that there are a lot of uncomfortably fat people on the streets, as there undeniably are. They don't take any notice – if they listen at all – because you insist on calling it obesity, which sounds like something you catch and can't be blamed for. If you want them to listen – and I'm not sure you do although you have to be seen trying – tell them they're fat, like we used to. However, they are not a time bomb. No matter how fat they get they will not explode. They will, though, die nice and early, and the cost to the NHS for the short time that they are alive will be more than compensated for by the much reduced bill for pensions, so don't worry.

* * * *

Things are a bit better now that I live off camp, have a home to go to. Only problem is I have to keep moving home. I get nicely settled in and then I get posted. This time it's to the Far East, which at least should be useful if not exciting. A bit of the Orient, a taster for future more exotic experiences, a chance to find out how I might get on with the natives when I really get going, a chance to learn the odd word or two of the kinds of language I might need. Mind you, there's only penguins at the South Pole.

Anyway, I'm not so sure about that South Pole business now. I've just read Slocum's book. He was the first to sail round the world single-handed, more like my kind of thing now I think about it. Reckon I can put up with the odd dowsing out there on the high seas — it'll be dry a lot of the time. And warm. I never was sure about weeks on end of the sub-zero stuff and the chance of losing my toes, which it seems is what regularly happens to even the toughest. That can happen on Everest, too. This solo circumnavigation thing would be more up my street. When I get out of this, of course.

I can't do anything about anything yet though, there's still six years of my sentence to run. And I've got other things to think about now I'm married, what with kids and that — there's one already on the way. Seems an irresponsible thing to do, just bugger off and leave Margaret to fend for herself. Makes you see Scott and his kind in a different light.

* * * *

There's been an accident just down the road from here. Someone's been killed, hit a lamp post. Saw it on the way to the shops today, all bent over and piled high with bunches of flowers and messages of sympathy. Robin apparently. **RIP Robin**. Sad, a little boy I suppose because there's a teddy-bear in the pile, though lots of grown-ups have teddy-bears these days, something to hang onto when times are bad for those who haven't got Chopin.

I was on my way to get my weekly fish and chips. Always have them on Friday. Nothing religious, just habit. Helps me to keep a handle on the week. Wheelie-bin on Wednesday, fish and chips on Friday. Know where I am then. No, nothing religious. Anyway, what kind of fool believes there's a spooky something out there telling them they've got to eat fish on Friday or nasty things will happen to them when they're dead? or for that matter they've got to grow a beard? or not cut their hair? or, for god's sake, slice their foreskin off? Show's what a fat lot of good universal education has been. All those years on the school bench and they still come out and cut their kid's foreskin off, surely chargeable as GBH. A while ago it occurred to me I ought to have my fish and chips on another day, as a kind of protest. Then I thought no, that's giving in, cowardice.

There was a different crew serving in the fish-and-chippery. I've not seen any of them before. Didn't see anyone I knew in the queue either. Must be something special about today, because the programmes on TV that I usually watch on Fridays seem to have been shifted too.

* * * *

"We seem to be well down the league table in the EU when it comes to education. What's the answer, Frank?"

Is that bad? Does it matter? Are we in some kind of competition? Get yourself an atlas from the nineteen-thirties, or thereabouts. You'll notice a third of the world's land mass is coloured pink. That was the British Empire. The coffers were overflowing. Now, thanks to education, we're all much cleverer. And bankrupt. We still do have the odd non-productive and very distant island, but you can hardly call that Empire. There may, of course, be no connection. Well worth feeding it into any computer model you may be using to plan all our futures, however.

* * * *

A lot's happening. Don't quite know where I am. Never got to grips with the Far East. We were in Singapore but not for long. I got this thing called Singapore Ear, incurable in a very humid climate apparently, so they sent us home. Now they're going to discharge me. Isn't this what I've been looking forward to for ten years?

I've a wife and baby daughter to support. It's come as a shock. Where do I go to do what? Christ knows. Much like coming out of prison I suppose – I've heard that employers look on ex-Servicemen in a similar light. I've applied for jobs, had interviews, one in Bristol, a couple in the Midlands. Nerve-wracking. After ten years concentrated depersonalisation, being treated not only as a person but as a person who might be wanted, was an alien concept. Don't know how I got on. In the meantime I'm on the dole.

At least the ear's better. The humidity in Singapore often topped a hundred percent in cloudless conditions. Humidity is supposed to be a measurement of the amount of moisture in the air, so by my simple, apparently unscientific, reasoning at a hundred percent it ought to have been chucking it down. But I must say I rather like the idea that there might be no connection between the measured amount of moisture in the air and the actual amount of water in the air. I mean, if you're trapped in a raging blizzard or forty-foot waves are breaking over the prow, humidity might still be low, which sounds like good news if you're the adventurous sort and you've got ears that respond badly to a touch of humidity. You see, I've still got plans, even if I've got to wait a bit for the opportunity.

* * * *

Spent most of the day on a wasted trip to the crematorium. It was Alan, the chap who worked at the hospital, showed people where to go. Adrian, not Alan. The service was supposed to be at two-fifteen but when I got there I didn't recognize anyone and the name on the board was Hitchcock. Couldn't remember Adrian's name but it wasn't Hitchcock – I'm sure that's what it said on the board but I'd got the wrong glasses, a mix-up with the old ones which I forgot to throw away. I've got six pairs in the drawer now and haven't a clue what's what. Anyway it turned out that Adrian's funeral is tomorrow, Tuesday. I thought today was Tuesday. Don't know how that happened. No wonder the TV has been all over the place. Songs of Praise on a Saturday didn't seem right. If I'd had a newspaper I might have noticed but I haven't been for one lately, had trouble walking.

Went into town a week back with my shoes on the wrong feet and didn't notice till I came to take them off back home. Now I've got sores.

Came as a shock, Adrian snuffing it. He's the chap who used to show people round at the hospital. Fit as a fiddle. Ran marathons. Never went to see a doctor. Collapsed, out jogging in the park, a couple of kids found him lying in the bushes. I can't think how he got into the bushes – not the sort of place jogging is likely to take you to, is it? The post-mortem said it was a heart attack. Sixty-seven he was, a youngster.

Could've done without the wasted journey. It's not just my feet – this morning I had to crawl to the bathroom to get the ibu-whateveritis. Lumbago, like being kicked in the back by a mule. Took me the best part of the morning to get upright. Well, nearly upright. Upright's not easy these days, not like it was when I was being marched everywhere. I spent ten years of my life being marched about, upright. Being upright was the only bit I never quite flushed out of my system. It could've been worse. A year or two back some of the men I was marched about with had a re-union celebrating their enlistment, sixty years on, the cretins. You see how the system can get you if you don't watch out. Take a long look at those poor old sods on parade at the Stenograph.

Now it's back tomorrow, to the crematorium. Seen four go up in smoke already this year. Three. Three or four. Anyway, several. A couple last year as well. Perhaps they should open a bar there, for us regulars. Ho. Burning's all the rage these days, over and done with in less time than it takes to eat a prawn cockerel, and you don't have to hang around. My daughter – she lives down south, comes up to visit when she can – thinks it's best, but what would I like. I said it'll be your problem, deal with it to suit yourself. When she asked me what I would want doing with my ashes I told her to put them in Margaret's knicker drawer, they'd be at home there. Haven't got rid of any of her clothes. Can't. She might come back.

Cenotaph. That's what I meant. They put it up to make us remember, so we wouldn't make the same mistake again. Ho.

She isn't coming back, is she? Sod it.

* * * *

"For a man of your age you're still very fit and active Frank. It would help if more people were like you. We'd like you to consider helping us develop a national fitness campaign based on your regime. How about it?"

Campaign? Regime? Are we going to war? Getting rid of another someone we don't like? No, I'm sure what you mean is you'd like me to let you into the secrets of my diet, exercise and excretal routines. Sorry, I don't have any. Wouldn't be of use to anybody anyway if they didn't have the same input at conception. The drip-feed of NHS advancements might help to keep them alive a bit longer than mum, dad or both. That's about it.

* * * *

Quite like Sheffield. Didn't fancy the idea of North at first, but you have to take work where you find it. The Excalibur Pump & Pipe Co. doesn't pay great money, but boasts it hasn't had to lay anyone off in the last forty years and has a good pension scheme. We get Christmas parties too, for the kids. They've got a walking club for families, Sundays once a month, and we take our daughter.

Kinder Scout – that mysterious place I once thought I might hone my embryo Everest skills on – is just up the road. I've been up it a few times with our walking group. It's about two-thousand feet, a pimple really, you can't even call it a mountain. I suppose it is a bit mysterious, lots of very messy, very deep wet peat bog, and you could easily get lost in fog, get stuck – someone died of hypothermia up there last year – and there are supposed to be bits of aeroplanes still around from those mysterious disappearances during the war I remember reading about. But it's a popular outing for the hiking people round here, always has been, although there was a bit of do about that before the war.

Anyway, I'm not too sure about Everest now because I've found out that I'm not very good at heights and likely to get in a tangle with ropes. And to be a mountaineer I think I should've started earlier. The Pole's still on my list – you just have to be able to walk, pull a sledge and put up with a bit of cold. I'm more inclined to the sailing round the world thing though. In fact I've joined a local sailing club. If you're going to sail round the world you need to learn how to jibe, and what a kedge warp is, that sort of thing.

They only race round buoys in a disused gravel pit but it'll be a start.

* * * *

Ibuprofen. That's it. It used to be aspirin. Or Sloane's liniment. Cured anything. Don't think you can get it any more, Sloanes. Had a picture of an old geezer with a moustache on the label.

The nurse comes three times a week to dress the ulcer in my foot. Don't know how but a few weeks ago I managed to get my shoes on the wrong feet. Walked into town, and didn't notice till I got back and came to take them off. I thought it was odd that they were uncomfortable because they'd never been uncomfortable before. Anyway I got sores and one of them's developed into an ulcer, a big hole, weeping. Nasty. The only shoes I can wear are some deck shoes that are falling to bits. I can't walk far and carry things, so I've had to get myself a shopping trolley and a stick, a tricky business. The walking group are very helpful, getting me to the pub to join them for the follow-up meal. There's four of us now who only go for the dinner.

Whatsisname was whisked up the chimney in front of a good crowd. Adrian, the chap who I used to work with and showed people where to go to at the hospital. Julian, who lives opposite and used to dig up roads, took me. It turned out Julian's wife Rita was Adrian's sister-in-law, or brother's sister-in-law, something like that. Sad didn't come easy because Rita has great legs and was a bit of a distraction in black stockings.

Someone got up and told us all about Alan but I hadn't got my hearing aids – I've forgotten where I keep the batteries, and they won't let me have any more at the surgery because they've only just given me the lot I can't find. From the bits I could make out though, like everybody else he was an especially fine and helpful fellow with a loving family, but distinguished from the rest of us by having once built a kitchen worktop perpendicular. I think that's what they said though I'm not sure about the worktop thing – I hadn't got my hearing aids. I remember him as getting in a tangle with one of the directors' secretaries, and as an occasional drunk.

If people are going to say nice things about me they can say them now, not wait until I'm dead.

Worktop peninsular, that was it.

* * * *

"What are we to do about this binge drinking culture, Frank, all this cheap booze. It's out of control. Town centres are disaster areas Friday and Saturday nights, crowds of legless drunks running amok, A&Es overwhelmed. What can we do?"

Well you might like to declare us a Muslim state. A bit

drastic that, and you could find that there are other far nastier ways of coping with the disappointing and largely failed lives most of us lead, if you get my drift. And are you sure you won't be joining the weekend's grand piss-up with the rest of us when after the next election you find yourself down at the job-centre? Oblivion is a smashing place. Have you ever been there?

Leave us be. Just hose down the streets and carry away any bodies the morning after.

By the way, when you're legless it's very unlikely you'll be able to run, amok or otherwise. A small point but not altogether without import.

* * * *

I held on to my job when the Excalibur Pump & Pipe Co. went down the tubes last year and we were restructured. The new management team decided we were too last-century, so we've been given a makeover and we're now Excalibur Logistics. Not sure what's different, we're still making the same stuff. My daughter thinks the Logistics bit must be something to do with the spanking brand new fleet of liveried vehicles we're now shuffling up and down the motorways. She's away at university now, down south.

Didn't get on with the sailing club. Most clubs have a President but it seems in sailing clubs you have a Commodore. I spent a lot of years developing a deep dislike for Commodores and their ilk, so I wasn't going to put up with that nonsense. It was an even bet there were more of the braided bastards lurking amongst the club's hierarchy. I did learn enough to get myself round a buoy but if I'm going to make it round the world I'll need a whole lot more than a lee-ho. Like how to survive for days on end at an angle of forty-five degrees. Anyway, a bloke named Wally has just made the first unsupported crossing of the North Pole. What more inspiration could I want? With a name like that he's clearly one of my sort, and I wouldn't mind coming in second.

And there's something else. For my forty-fifth birthday Margaret bought me an ancient edition of Charles Doughty's Travels in Arabia Deserta. Wow. Got me hooked. Another one of those unlikely Victorian wanderers reared to believe there was a whole heap more to them than ordinary mortal stock provides. It's an idea. If it did come to a toss-up between the Pole and, say, the Empty Quarter, I reckon a crotchety camel and a touch of sunburn beats losing your toes to frostbite any day.

* * * *

"People aren't happy with all these Johnny Foreigners coming over here, Frank. They say it should be British jobs for British people, but British people don't seem to want the jobs. How do we get round this one?"

Johnny Foreigners? A bit out of date aren't we? Still, now that the more definitive terms we used to use are out of bounds, perhaps you'll get away with that one.

To the point. Of course people don't want jobs. Jobs are what those at the bottom of the heap do, scratching a living by whatever means they can including burglary –

house jobs, inside jobs, that sort of thing. And since our education system is designed to ensure everyone has a doctorate by 2050, it's pretty clear that the concept of jobs for the home-grown has a limited future. So do nothing. Pretty soon, as the rubbish builds up in the streets, buses grind to a halt, the old have to wipe their own bums and restaurants and fast-food outlets disappear faster than snow in the Sahara, they'll all begin to recognise what jolly fine people these Johnny Foreigners are.

* * * *

In hospital. Didn't hear the car until the last minute – I still haven't found my hearing aid batteries – and I couldn't see it properly. It's these catacombs, cataclysms – those eye things, my optician says they're doing nicely. Like looking through gauze. Cataracts. I'll have to think of those rough bits you get in rivers. Anyway, trying to get out of the way of the car I got in a tangle with my stick and shopping trolley, fell over one of those out-front coffee tables, fractured my pelvis.

My consultant's name is Sid. Doesn't fill you with a lot of confidence does it? Actually his name is Siddiqi, but I call him Sid. I call him Sid because like everyone else here he insists on calling me Frank. Don't know where all this chummy stuff came from. You have to go along with it though, it doesn't do to stand out when you're helpless. Still I like to keep them on their toes, the nurses. Have you had your bowels open today, Frank? Bowels open?

For god's sake it's the twenty-first century, woman, and I'm not a bloody child. If I can't crap I'll let you know. They're a bit wary of me now.

There's still a hole in my foot. Apparently it's because I have diabetes. Don't know where that came from, never have sugar in my tea. They tell me that if they can't get this ulcer thing cleared up they may have to take my foot off. Christ! I mean, if it'd been frostbite picked up on the way to the Pole I could take that. Or if I'd had to hack it off with a penknife when trapped under a dead camel crossing the Sahara solo. All I did was walk into town with my shoes on the wrong bloody feet.

My daughter came up to see me a couple of days ago. She lives down south. It's a long way to come and she's getting on a bit. She says when I come out of hospital I'll need some help, someone to do the shopping, see to the garden. I really ought to think about going into sheltered housing. There's some very nice apartments, Sunset Court, near the shops and there's a bus-stop right outside. Sunset Court? – it's full of helpless old farts on their way out, I tell her. And they're flats.

My consultant Sid, Siddiqi, tells me it'll be some time before I'll be able to think about walking far. As he's a consultant I suppose I should call him Mr. Sid. We all have consultants now. It used to be only rich people had consultants, the rest of us had doctors. Same with apartments. Only rich people had apartments. The rest of us had flats.

* * * *

For a retirement present the chaps at Excalibur Fluid Transfer Solutions bought me some hedge trimmers and a book about a woman who retired and cycled round the world. Now that's more like it. I used to like cycling, and it didn't look like there'd be a lot of organising to do or expense involved. What's more even pensioners can do it apparently. Mind you, I wouldn't mind being the first pensioner to get to the Pole – either end will do – on foot. Haven't got any further with the sailing, so it looks like all that round-the-Horn-under-canvas stuff is out. And that Empty Quarter thing – never really was on. Animals don't get on with me, and camels can be particularly nasty as I found out in the sand dunes on a package holiday in the Canaries.

Anyway I've now bought myself a bike. It's got twenty-seven gears. Don't know what you do with all that lot – in my day we rode fixed – but it should get me up any mountain that gets in my way. Haven't ridden a bike for forty years and it's a bit tricky, can't cock my leg over like I used to for one thing, and I lose my nerve when faced with narrow gaps so that I bump into things. I'll soon get the hang of it though. By this time next year I'll be ready. Margaret says if I don't do it now it may be too late, because at our age you don't know what's around the corner.

Our neighbour Derrick – we go out for a drink together Saturday lunchtimes – thinks I must be mad to risk getting mixed up with all those funny foreigners, most of whom, he tells me, can't be trusted, you only have to read the papers. I think he means the Daily Mail. He really is a Derrick which someone ought to have told his parents is a kind of swivelling crane, named after a

What the hell is a Bede? Or was there only one? There must have been more for one of them to be venerable, mustn't there?

* * * *

Not used to living on my own. It's not something our generation knows anything about. We all stayed at home until we got married. There were always other people around. If I don't go out I've got no one to talk to. It was never like that before. Ever. Margaret never went to the doctor's. She said if it ain't broke, don't fix it.

She's not gone really. The door will open any minute and she'll be here again. A year on that's how it still feels because she's always been here. She's part of the house, our house. People expect me to call it my house. I can't do that. They say they know how I feel. No they don't. We held each other tight some part of every day. Not long ago I was going to cycle round the world. Got all the gear, even worked out a start date so I didn't get the worst weather anywhere. Planned to go through all those Stans slotted in between Turkey and China. Then I realised I couldn't live for a month without her, let alone the year it would take me.

At first I didn't go out, stayed at home and got drunk, played the piano a lot. One day I threw the bike in the canal, but knew I'd gone too far – Derrick helped me to fish it out next day. Now I go down to the shops most days to get a newspaper. I've swapped some of the booze for coffee, and on good days I sit outside with a cappuccino (I like the little sprinkle of chocolate you get on top), see quite a lot of people I know even though some of them dodge out of my way. Least I think they do. Like when you've got a terminal illness, they don't know what to say. But it's the only way I get to speak to anyone, there and in The Comet. Not a proper name for a pub is it?

* * * *

"We know this isn't a good time for you Frank, but we really do need……….."

You're right, this isn't a good time. And there won't be any more good times, ever. So sod off.

* * * *

You can guess what they're saying about me down there, in Hove, my daughter.

"We've got Dad into sheltered housing. It's the best thing for him after that business with his hip. He won't have anything to do with those red handles he can pull to alert the warden, so we bought him a mobile phone. We've tried to show him how to use it but he doesn't listen, you know him. Nothing's changed. He can't hear properly anyway because he can't get batteries for his hearing aids, or he says he can't. I'm sure he could if he went to the doctor.

I don't think he gets on very well with the other residents. Well, he looks a bit of a tramp with that old camel stick he bought at the antiques fair when he thought he might be doing something in the desert, and in those old deck sandals – they're falling apart. I've suggested some smart trainers but he says he's not going training for anything. And you know how he used to try and play all that classical stuff on the piano – well, he's started up again and a lot of them are complaining. The warden's a bit concerned."

Well, if they don't like it, tough. I'm quite attached to those deck shoe things. Used to wear them at the sailing club until the Commodore said he'd put me on janks for being improperly dressed. I told him to get stuffed, as all his sort should. OK, so it didn't really happen – I made it up – but I'd like to think it did. And that camel stick, it's just the job for whacking pigeons when they get in my way in town. When it's warm I like to sit outside in the market place with a cappuccino, looking at ladies' legs, and these pigeons come pecking around so I whack them with my stick. The other day a lady said I was cruel. She said I shouldn't do that to Mother Carey's Chickens. I told her they weren't Mother Carey's anything, they were a bloody nuisance. And anyway Mother Carey's Chickens, I informed her, are stormy petrels, not pigeons.

* * * *

THE FAT LADY SINGS

This place is called Blackside, Blackside House. I call it Backside, an arsehole of a place. Can't stand the company, they're all barmy or brain dead. And the staff? Global village stuff, straight out of the kraal, the sampan and the tepee. Ho. I shouldn't joke like that, should I? Salt of the earth really, if you like salt. Can't say the same about the patronising bastards in charge who've told them to keep us exercised by patting balloons about. When they patted it to me I stuck a pin in it. That told them. They called me a spoilsport. I laughed.

I don't know how I got here. Someone from the flats must've complained. OK, so I left the gas on. Once. Just a one-off, I'm not losing it. And that piddle on the floor in the communal lounge – an accident. Happens to all of us, doesn't it? Still, it doesn't surprise me. They're a miserable lot at Sunset bloody Court. Were. No, still are I expect. Why should they become unmiserable just because I'm not there any more?

A woman called Valkyrie from the SS came and asked a lot of silly questions. I think it was probably Valerie from the Social Services but my glasses are all over the place and the print on her badge was a bit small. Could I look after myself? Was I eating? I said no, just sucking a mint imperial. Ho. That's what old people do I told her, suck mint imperials. Had I got any relatives who could look after me? If not I might have to be put in a home. I told her I was already in a home, mine. And no, I'd only got my daughter and she lives down south and thinks I ought to go into a home anyway. For your own good, she says. What she means is that it's for her good. Quite right too. Doesn't owe me anything. I'm not buying into that load of kid's-responsibility crap. I'm responsible for myself. I decide. I make my own decisions. So I said I'm not going to be put in a home by anyone. If I'm going into a home I'll put myself in it.

Of course it doesn't quite work like that. They came for me anyway, brought me here in a taxi.

* * * *

"What on earth are we going to do about all these millions of old people we seem to have, Frank? We really can't afford them. Their children should be responsible, but they don't seem to see it that way at all any more, not like they used to."

My, we have got hold of some quaint folklore, haven't we? You really think that the kids used to *want* to look after their parents? A myth, chaps, put about by governments hoping to get away with looking after us on the cheap.

Like I keep telling you, hold your nerve because there soon won't be any old people to worry about. In this age of NOW death is the only thing today's up-and-coming lot are prepared to wait for, but that I suggest is only temporary. And out there, waiting in the wings, is the next big thing in viruses, unhindered by immune systems long since distanced from anything approaching a bit of dirt.

* * * *

Thought you'd escaped, didn't you Frank? Thought we wouldn't be able to track you down? Oh no. Here at RAF Pentonville, we never lose anybody…….

Dear Frank,
Did you realise that this year marks our Entry's seventieth anniversary? It seems only like yesterday, doesn't it? I'm organising a little get-together at the Chiltern Pastures Home-from-Home where I'm currently in residence after a slight stroke. I was lucky to get in here – there's quite a waiting list. I can actually see my old billet from the bathroom window.

I say a little get-together because there's not many of us left now, in fact as far as I can find out there's only you and me. Sadly it looks like all the other one-hundred-and-ninety three have fallen by the wayside, gone to that great airfield in the sky, as you might like to say. I look forward to your reply.

   Your Comrade in Arms,
      J. Sprink Wg.Cdr. OBE

Dear Mr. Sprank
So we're an oboe, are we? You can be a bloody piccolo for all I care, you're still nuts. Soon enough you'll be celebrating the anniversary of the day you entered the Nursing Home. Good luck to you old chap, but I won't be with you or any other of the old lags you might trawl in for the seventieth piss-up. More likely I'll have a piss-up of my own, and lash out at anyone who calls themselves Wg Cdr.

PS Sorry about the stroke. The dementia, too. But that's the territory we're in now.

* * * *

There's a man here who thinks God is a potato. They all laugh at him. I tell them that it's quite possible that God is a potato. I tell them that God can be anything you choose, that if horses could draw they'd draw their gods like horses. The same surely goes for potatoes. They won't speak to me now.

I got that from somewhere – that thing about horses.

This place is called Blackside. I call it Backside. Ho. Stinks, but after a while you don't notice. You can't miss the expression on visitor's faces though. My daughter came up to see me last week. She lives down south. I used to live down there, during the war. Which war was that, you ask. Well, there was the First World War, called a world war because the whole of Europe was involved. A bit later there was The War, which was the one I spent some time in. Anyway, she remarked on it, the stink. My daughter, that is. Lives down south, Hove. Hove to, down south. Ho. She said I had the money, I could move somewhere else. I told her all the somewhere-elses were full of old people, just like here, and old people dripped wherever they were, even in Hove. She can't come up often to see me, my daughter. It's a long way, and she's getting on a bit.

A priest came round the other day. If we wanted to hear him would we gather in the lounge. I went along for the challenge. A waste of time really. Not exactly the intellectual elite, are they? Usual cobblers. He said he would pray for us. I suggested that since the unequivocal evidence from several thousand years of praying to his God is that it yields no results beyond calculable chance, what on earth made him think it was going to change now? That's what I meant to say, anyway, and I think I did. He said he'd seen all those crutches thrown away at Lourdes. So I asked him if he'd seen any prophetic limbs thrown away. Prospectic limbs. Prophylactic. Can't think of the word. Bugger it. Wooden legs, only they don't make them of wood any more. He just laughed, thought I was joking. I said if his God could make people walk again he could make them grow a new leg. He said he'd love to have a discussion with me sometime but he'd got other places to visit.

At mealtimes I sit with a chap called Barrington. He was a solicitor's clerk and wrote birthday-card poetry. He farts a lot, and nobody else wants to sit with him. Not fond of farting people myself, but you could say it was appropriate for a place named Backside. It's Blackside really, only Barrington and me, we call it Backside. Anyway, at least he keeps his mouth shut when eating and doesn't dribble. You can like him for that in here.

My daughter came up to see me last week. She said the place was awfully smelly. Don't notice myself, I'm used to it. Then again if you're a contributor you're not likely to admit it, are you?

* * * *

"We seem to have lost our moral compass, Frank. In a world now dedicated to the sole pursuit of personal pleasure we have surrendered our innate sense of the spiritual to the material. Faith is out of fashion. We believe in nothing that we cannot prove. Any ideas?"

Is that you, Canterbury? Still wearing that funny outfit are we? Only the bone through the nose is missing. Or perhaps the bells that are supposed to go with the cap. Whichever, vesti la giubba, on with the mottley. I too once donned the mottley. We called it a uniform. Serge it was, coarse and scratchy, not like yours which I'll bet is made of the finest silk.

About that moral compass thing – it's a bit different to the magnetic one old chap. Where it points to depends very much on whose hands it's in – there's no moral north pole, no universal absolute, in which case it can't be lost. And faith out of fashion? I'm not so sure – there's still enough of it around to get you blown to bits. As for spirit, it comes in bottles and gets you stoned. Now there's a thought, if you're right after all – that it goes on after I'm dead – book me in.

* * * *

There's this lady here – you can see that she once had nice legs. Well, I can. I suggested we could get together sometime. And very, very soon. Had we but world enough and time – I quoted Marvell right down to that bit about the grave being a fine and private place but none, I thought, did there embrace. She said she didn't know what on earth I was talking about. Andrew Marvell, I said, to his coy mistress. Is that the chap over there in the corner, she asked, the one with the sticking plaster on his glasses and the catheter bag? Andrew Marvell, the poet, I shouted. I remember *Captain* Marvel, she said, and you don't have to shout.

gets you, and they're thick with fleas that lot.

Bridlington – the chap I sit with at mealtimes – says you have to stick up for yourself. When they patted a balloon in my direction I stuck a pin in it. That showed them.

* * * *

Didn't get up this morning. Couldn't. Didn't want to. Not easy when you've only got one foot. Nicola – the black girl – came in and asked me if there was anything I wanted. Of course there was, black, yellow, purple, any colour you like, but it's a bloody long time since I could've done anything about it. Ho. So I asked if it was Tuesday and if it was would she put the bin out for me. She said it was Saturday and it was time I stopped worrying about the bins, it was all done for me now, and had I had my medication? Which one was that? Last time I counted there was fifteen bloody bits of the stuff. Anyway, I don't care, not bothered, not bothered. I'll die if I do, I'll die if I don't. This place is a morgue anyway, I'm the only one still breathing, and a good job too otherwise there'd be no one to put the bin out, except Niagra or whatever her name is, the black girl. Dennis, next door, used to put it out for me, but he's gone now. Didn't like foreigners or cats, Dennis. Derrick. Dennis is a big lorry. Derrick is a swivelling thing, a crane.

There's Germans outside, in the grounds. Saw them out the window. Nobody's chasing them off. Know why I know they're Germans? They've got square heads, my

EDITOR'S NOTE

No one knows for sure how long Frank was left out there. Barrington, a colleague at Blackside House, says he took him out on Tuesday – he's certain of this because it was bin day, as he called it. This was quite possible because he was first reported missing on the Wednesday morning but, as is now well known, Frank wasn't discovered until Saturday. Whatever the true circumstances it was fortunate for us that he kept his notebook in a plastic bag, a little chewed round the edge where the badger (or whatever it was) had taken the lump out of his leg, but untouched by the rain during those last hours. His final jottings are clearly legible. Never one to mince his words Frank, like many in old age, felt less concern to avoid offence, and some minor editorial interventions in his later notes was felt necessary.

GLOSSARY

The graph representing progress is exponential and, in Frank's lifetime, was already approaching the vertical, so that many of his references were passing into history even as he wrote. A glossary, he thought, would come in handy. In time the glossary expanded to include other references which he thought might be useful. *Editor*

A

Abraham – father of the Hebrew nation/ religion. Frank is not at all clear why anyone should want a father prone to fantasies about sacrificing his son (see Isaac), but he accepts that there are some funny people about.

Aids, hearing – date back to the ear-trumpet which has been around a good deal longer than Frank. Although aids in current use are much more discreet, the presence of a deaf old duffer can still be easily detected by the feedback whistle.

AWOL – Absent Without Leave, fancy name for desertion from duty in the armed services. For this, in ancient times you could be strung up. Not so long ago you would be shot. In today's more understanding world you will probably be counselled and sent home to Mummy.

B

Blackside – Blackside House, a totally invented name for a Nursing Home for the helpless elderly somewhere in England.

Barrington – mealtime companion of Frank at Blackside. Sometimes referred to as Basingstoke, Battersea, Billingsgate or Bridlington.

Bede, The Venerable – 7/8th-century scholar from Jarrow (the North, which see) responsible for the first history of the English peoples. Although the title implies the existence of unvenerable Bedes, Frank was unable to verify this.

Bin – wheelie-bin, dustbin on wheels

Bin day – the day on which the wheelie-bin collection takes place. A useful starting point for establishing the weekly routine of those not in work, for whom Monday has no significance

C

Cappuccino – a coffee drink, originating from Italy according to most authorities, prepared in a manner intended to give the appearance of shaving soap, and sprinkled with chocolate dust sometimes patterned. It is usually obtainable in three sizes – small (large), regular (even larger), and large (served in a receptacle huge enough to require two handles).

Coronation Street – popular, and interminable, TV fictional account of the lives of a group of everyday northern folk, none of whom show the slightest interest in anything at all. Excepting, possibly, themselves.

Crematorium – a building designed for the controlled burning of the deceased, bonfires now being considered an environmental hazard.

D

Dennis – a big lorry. Also the occasional name of Frank's neighbour Derrick

Derrick – a swivelling crane. Also the birth name of

Frank's neighbour, properly named Derek.

E

Everest — world's highest mountain. Frank's early plans to be the first to conquer Everest were leaked, thereby enabling Edmund Hilary and Sherpa Tensing to beat him to it.

Excalibur Pump & Pipe Co. — later known as Excalibur Logistics and subsequently Excalibur Fluid Transfer Solutions. If this is, or ever has been, the name of a Sheffield company, Frank never worked there.

F

Fart, old — follower of a school of philosophy rooted in largely imagined past glories, excellence etc, sometimes referred to as the Laudatores Tempori Acti (Not-like-it-was-in-my-day) philosophy.

Frank — romanticist, would-be operatic tenor, concert pianist, mountaineer and explorer, yachtsman, poet, novelist and Royal Academy exhibitor. Excused duties on all counts, being a baritone with fat fingers, uncertain of heights and rough seas, with animals prone to attack on sight, and imbued with little natural literary or artistic talent.

O

Officer, officer classes – a self-perpetuating "posh boys" elite in British society, inherent believers in their own right to rule which, unlike the French version, has (so far) proved ineradicable.

P

Pharmacy – retailer of health products, may sometimes be referred to as "the Chemist's" by the elderly and others of the lower social orders

Pole – upright stick. Also, most northerly and southerly points of the planet – where the axes would stick out if there were any. Uninhabited, very, very cold and the devil of a job to get to.

Q

Quarter, Empty – believed by Frank to be part of Arabia with absolutely nothing in it apart from sand and cameldung

S

Scott – Sir Robert Falcon Scott. Aimed to be the first to reach the South Pole but made a mess of things, came in second and died on the return journey. This is considered, in true British tradition, a glorious failure which, also in true British tradition when achieved by a member of the Officer Classes (which see), guarantees a hero's status.

T

Tensing, Sherpa – Himalayan porter of rich mountaineers' bits and pieces, arguably the first man to top Mt Everest.

V

Valkyrie – mythical Teutonic tough bit of female goods, not the sort you'd want to meet on the hunt.

W

Wally – Wally Herbert, unsung British polar explorer who actually got there (more than once) and didn't die. May even have been the first to reach the North Pole. In failing to achieve a glorious failure, Wally also failed to achieve hero status, thereby ensuring he doesn't appear in The New Penguin Encyclopedia, unlike Scott (which see). His name probably didn't help, either.